KNIGH✝MARE

For Lucy, Theo and Tara – PB

For Mum and Dad, who encouraged
my scribbling from the beginning – FB

STRIPES PUBLISHING
An imprint of Little Tiger Press
1 The Coda Centre, 189 Munster Road,
London SW6 6AW

A paperback original
First published in Great Britain in 2014

Text copyright © Peter Bently, 2014
Illustrations copyright © Fred Blunt, 2014

ISBN: 978-1-84715-434-7

The right of Peter Bently and Fred Blunt to be identified as the
author and illustrator of this work respectively has been asserted
by them in accordance with the Copyright, Designs and Patents Act, 1988.

Printed and bound in the UK.

10 9 8 7 6 5 4 3 2 1

KNIGHTMARE

Feast Fight!

PETER BENTLY

Illustrated by Fred Blunt

Stripes

CEDRIC'S WORLD

CASTLE BOMBAST

Sir Percy the Proud

Cedric
Thatchbottom
(Me!)

Patchcoat the Jester

Margaret the Cook

BLACKSTONE FORT

Sir Roland the Rotten

Walter Warthog

SPIFFINGTON MANOR

Algernon Whympleigh

Sir Spencer the Splendid

Chapter One

An Arrowing Experience

SWISH!

"*Eeeek!*"

THUNK! TWOINNNG!

"Ah, I think we'll call that a warm-up shot, Cedric," said Sir Percy, lowering his bow. "Now be a good fellow and fetch the arrow."

"Y-yes, Sir Percy."

I walked shakily to the large oak tree

and pulled out Sir Percy's arrow. It was *exactly* where I'd been standing just a few seconds earlier.

"Shift the target a bit to the left," he said. "Those trees are spoiling my line of sight."

"Yes, Sir Percy," I sighed. For the zillionth time that morning I lugged the target to a new spot. Sooner or later he might actually hit it. Just as long as he didn't hit me first.

"That's better," said Sir Percy. "And don't stand so close to it. It puts me off my aim."

I *hadn't* been standing close the last time. I'd been sheltering somewhere nice and safe — or so I'd thought. If I hadn't dived out of the way, Sir Percy would have needed a new squire for the second time in three months.

KNIGHTMARE

A knight is supposed to teach his squire proper knighting skills. But somehow my master – known to his many fans as Sir Percy the Proud – never quite gets round to it. Just like that morning, when he'd said he *might* let me have a go with the bow once he'd "warmed up". Two hours of "warm-up shots" later I obviously wasn't going to be firing my first arrow any time soon. I can safely say that Sir Percy couldn't hit a castle gate if it was right in front of his nose.

Actually, make that a *castle*.

Could this really be the same famous knight who once shot a secret message tied to an arrow through the arrow-slit of a besieged castle? From half a mile away?

KNIGHTMARE

At night? Blindfolded? It's one of the best bits of *The Song of Percy*, Sir Percy's wildly popular account of his knightly deeds. Hmmm. It wasn't the first time I'd wondered whether *The Song of Percy* might be a bit … exaggerated.

He notched another arrow to his bow and I quickly checked for a safe place to fling myself the moment he fired.

"Ready, Cedric?"

"Ready, Sir Percy."

All of a sudden I heard the sound of hooves among the trees. But before I could say anything, a gust of wind blew Sir Percy's dashing new green and orange velvet hunting cap over his eyes.

TWANGGG!

"Bother!"

Sir Percy fired blindly into the air.

I leaped for cover, but luckily his arrow flew high over the trees.

"Blasted breeze!" said Sir Percy, pushing the cap off his eyes. "Ah, well. No harm d—"

"Aaargh!"

There was a startled yell and a whinny. Then a grandly dressed man rode out of the trees looking alarmed – and very cross. Sir Percy's arrow was sticking out of his saddle, right between his legs. A couple of inches the wrong way and ... ouch!

"This is an outrage!" roared the rider, who looked vaguely familiar. "Raining arrows on me. I could have been cut off in my prime!"

"My sincerest apologies," said Sir Percy. "It was the wind."

"I don't care about your personal problems," said the man. He yanked the arrow out of his saddle and flung it at Sir Percy's feet. "Next time, mind where you're shooting, you careless twerp!"

"Now look here," scowled Sir Percy, puffing out his chest. "I will have you know that I, Sir Percy Piers Peregrine de Bluster de Bombast, will not be spoken to in that tone by the likes of-of—"

"Fitztightly," fumed the man. "Baron Buskin Fitztightly. Chief Herald of

KNIGHTMARE

His Majesty the King. And good morning to you, Sir Percy."

Sir Percy's face quickly switched to his cheesiest grin. It was better than one of Patchcoat the jester's conjuring tricks.

"Ah, my *dear* Baron Fitztightly!" declared Sir Percy, doffing his cap and sweeping an impressively smarmy bow.

KNIGHTMARE

"Just my little joke! Of course I recognized you at once," he fibbed. "*Delighted* to see your lordship. You are most welcome to Castle Bombast. And how *is* His Majesty? In fine health, I trust?"

"You can ask him yourself," said Baron Fitztightly. "At the banquet tomorrow night."

"A royal banquet?" said Sir Percy. "How simply marvellous! Cedric, we must prepare to travel to the palace at once. I shall need new evening robes, my best armour, a new set of plumes for my helmet, and—"

"This *isn't* an invitation to the palace," interrupted the baron.

"Oh," said Sir Percy. "So who's throwing the banquet?"

"*You* are," said the baron.

"Wh-what?" spluttered Sir Percy. "*Me?* Y-you mean the king is coming *here?*"

"Indeed," said the baron. "The king and queen are visiting every knight who did well in the tournament. Including *you*, Sir Percy. Or perhaps you'd forgotten?"

So *that's* where I'd seen Baron Fitztightly before! A few weeks earlier, the fearsome Sir Roland the Rotten had challenged Sir Percy to a joust at the king's tournament. Sir Percy wriggled out of it by making me wear his armour and pretend to be him.

Amazingly, I actually won the joust – by a sheer fluke. But of course everyone thought I was Sir Percy so he took all the credit.

KNIGHTMARE

He'd even had a huge, expensive tapestry made called *The Triumph of Sir Percy*. It shows Sir Percy knocking Sir Roland off his horse into a large pile of poop. And very splendid it looks, too – apart from the tiny detail that it never actually happened.

"Their Majesties expect your best bedchambers, an excellent banquet and top-notch entertainment," the baron went on. "They will arrive just in time to dine at seven o'clock. Talking of which, I'd better get on and deliver these invitations." He patted a leather bag with two parchment scrolls sticking out of it.

"Invitations?" said Sir Percy. "Who else is coming?"

"Whenever the king stays with one of his knights, he always invites all the other local knights to the banquet," said the baron.

"Oh, goody!" said Sir Percy. "That means he'll be inviting my old pal Sir Spencer the Splendid. He only lives an hour's ride away.

18

KNIGHTMARE

What fun!"

"Correct," said the baron. "I'm going there next."

"So who's that other invite for?" said Sir Percy. "Ah, I know!" He gave the baron a sly nod and a wink. "Is it perhaps for some noble young … lady? After all, there are no other knights around here."

"Depends what you mean by 'around here'," said the baron. "This district stretches as far as the Forest of Grimwood."

Sir Percy's face fell. "*Grimwood?*" he said. "But only one other knight lives between here and Grimwood, and that's … that's—"

"Sir Roland the Rotten," said the baron with a wry smile. "Precisely. I'm sure he'll

19

be *delighted* to come to the banquet. Good day, Sir Percy!"

"B-but your lordship!" spluttered Sir Percy. "Wait! I-I…"

But the baron had already ridden off at a brisk trot.

We set off back to the castle. Sir Percy hurried ahead while I staggered behind him carrying all his archery equipment.

"Do keep up, Cedric," grouched Sir Percy.

"Sorry, Sir Percy," I panted.

"We must start preparing at once for the royal visit," said Sir Percy. "There's a lot to arrange. However, it would be *most* unknightly to overburden one's squire, and therefore I'm only giving you three things to do."

"Thanks, Sir Percy," I said.

"Don't mention it, dear boy," said Sir Percy. "So you're in charge of the bedchambers, the banquet and the entertainment. I shall take care of – um – everything else."

"Er – *is* there anything else, Sir Percy?" I said before I could stop myself.

"*Most* amusing, Cedric," he frowned. "Kindly remember your Squire's Code and refrain from being cheeky to your master."

"Sorry, Sir Percy," I said.

"As a matter of fact I shall be *extremely* busy," Sir Percy said huffily. "But first we have to deal with Sir Roland. There's no way he's coming here to spoil *my* banquet. Besides, it'll be cheaper with one less guest to feed."

"How can you stop him?" I asked. "He's been invited by the king himself."

I hated the idea of Sir Roland coming as much as Sir Percy did – especially as he'd bring his sneaky squire, Walter Warthog. But I didn't see what Sir Percy could do about it.

22

KNIGHTMARE

"Simple, Cedric," said Sir Percy. "We must make sure Sir Roland never receives the king's invitation."

Uh-oh. I was starting to learn that when Sir Percy said something was "simple" it usually ended up being difficult and dangerous.

"But the baron's already on his way to Blackstone Fort," I said. Blackstone Fort is Sir Roland's huge scary castle and I still shiver to think about the time Sir Percy got me to sneak into it at night.

"Indeed, Cedric," said Sir Percy. "But he's heading to *Sir Spencer's* castle first. It's an hour away by the main road. If you cut through the wood on Gristle the mule you'll easily catch him up."

KNIGHTMARE

"Me?" I said.

"Of course, Cedric," said Sir Percy. "It'll be good practice for overtaking an enemy army. And then all you have to do is simply – um – retrieve the invitation from the baron."

"But Sir Percy!" I blurted. "Isn't that … *stealing?*"

"Nonsense!" said Sir Percy. "If Sir Roland never *has* his invitation, how can you *steal* it? Now go and saddle Prancelot for me. I have to pop into the village on – er – urgent banquet business. Hurry now!"

I was about to ask how I was supposed to take the invitation without the baron noticing, but Sir Percy had already loped off into the castle.

24

Chapter Two

Malarkey at the Manor

I stashed away the archery stuff in one of the castle cellars. Then I hurried to saddle Prancelot and Gristle. I was about to leave when Sir Percy came in with a large leather sack hoisted over his shoulder.

"Prancelot's all ready for you, Sir Percy," I said from behind the door.

"Oh!" he cried in alarm, dropping the

sack. It landed on the cobbled floor with a clang. "I thought you'd already left!"

"Sorry to startle you, Sir Percy," I said. "One of Gristle's stirrups was broken. I had to hunt for a spare. Here, let me pick that up."

"No!" said Sir Percy, hastily snatching up the sack and clutching it to his chest. "I mean, no – no need to bother, dear boy," he added breezily. "Anyway, hadn't you better be off?"

"Yes, Sir Percy," I said. I bowed and led Gristle from the stable. Sir Percy saw me out with a fixed smile. He was still standing there, clutching the sack and grinning at me over the stable door, as I rode across the courtyard and out of the castle. What was all that about?

KNIGHTMARE

I'd assumed that Sir Percy's "cut through the woods" was an actual path. But oh no. The only way to get to Spiffington Manor, Sir Spencer's castle, was through a thick tangle of trees and undergrowth. Before long Gristle refused to go on, so I tied him to a tree and continued on foot. When I finally saw the gates of Spiffington Manor I'd been battered by branches, shredded by shrubs and scratched to bits by brambles.

It had taken me an hour and a half and I was certain I'd missed the baron. As I walked up to the castle gates I saw a rider leaving, escorted by one of Sir Spencer's guards. But as I got closer, I saw it wasn't the baron at all but some kind of travelling merchant.

"We ain't interested," I heard the guard say. "Now clear off."

"But my Bottom-Boil Balsam is the best in the kingdom," said the merchant. "It cures all pains in the posterior!"

"I said clear off," barked the guard. "Now! Or I'll give *you* a pain in the posterior – with me pike!"

KNIGHTMARE

"Tell you what," said the merchant. "I'll leave you this leaflet with my special offers."

He handed a scroll of parchment to the guard – who just tossed it over his shoulder. The wind caught it and carried it off.

"I said *now*!" he glowered.

"All right, all right! Please yourself," said the merchant, riding across the drawbridge. As he passed me he said, "Good morning, young sir! Master Botolph's the name. And how is your bottom today?"

"Fine!" I said, and hurried to the gate.

"Halt!" said the guard. "If you're sellin' something then you can blinkin' well—"

Before he could finish, who should come striding out of the castle but Sir Spencer the

29

Splendid himself – with Baron Fitztightly!

"Great to see you, Fitznicely!" said Sir Spencer, slapping the baron on the back so hard that he almost fell down the steps. "And a big thumbs-up to His Maj for the cool invite. Now, are you sure you won't stay and see my collection of embroidered cloaks?"

"Er – no," said the baron, dodging another back-slap. "Thanks for the mug of mead but I must get going. Have someone fetch my horse from the stables, will you?"

I suddenly saw the perfect chance to get my hands on Sir Roland's invitation.

"I'll do it, sir!" I exclaimed.

The guard barred my way. "Oi, not so fast, sunshine!" he said.

KNIGHTMARE

"Whoa! Easy, Sergeant, easy!" said Sir Spencer. "This chap looks kind of familiar."

"I believe it's Sir Percy's squire," said the baron. "Didn't I see you earlier, lad?"

I bowed. "Yes, my lord."

"Of course!" said Sir Spencer, flashing me a dazzling smile. I'd never seen such amazing teeth. Hardly any of them were rotten and only one or two were missing. "I saw you at the tournament. Hold on, I never forget a name ... it's ... Cecil, right?"

"Um, *Cedric*, Sir Spencer."

"Er, yeah, I knew that!" he beamed, flicking his long golden locks out of his eyes. "So, Frederick, what brings you solo to Spencer Central?"

KNIGHTMARE

Yikes! I'd spent so long thinking about how to take the invite that I hadn't even thought of an excuse for my visit.

"Well, I-I..." I stammered. "Er – Sir Percy wants to know what you're wearing to the banquet. Um – just so you don't clash."

"Good man, good man!" said Sir Spencer. "Tell him I'm coming in my new green and orange velvet dinner tunic. Green and orange is *definitely* the new yellow and scarlet. Hey, baron, how about I show it to you before you go?"

"*No*," said the baron firmly. He turned to me. "Thank you for offering to fetch my horse, young man."

Sir Spencer pointed me towards the stables. With no one to see me, it was easy to slip the invitation out of the baron's saddlebag. But something bothered me. When the baron found the invitation was missing, wouldn't he simply *tell* Sir Roland about the banquet? Somehow I had to stop

33

KNIGHTMARE

the baron going to Blackstone Fort.
So much for Sir Percy's simple plan!

And then I spotted something just
outside the stable. It was the merchant's
scroll, lying on a pile of horse poo where
the guard had tossed it. Checking that no
one was looking, I snatched it up. *Hmm,*
I thought, flicking off a stray bit of poo.
I wonder…

I steadied the baron's horse as he swung
himself up into the saddle.

"And you're sure you don't fancy another
mug of mead?" said Sir Spencer.

"Certainly not," said the baron. "That

first one has made me rather sleepy. The last thing I feel like doing is riding up that hill to Blackstone Fort."

"Um – excuse me, your lordship?" I said.

The baron turned to me. "Yes, young man?"

"Perhaps you don't need to ride *all* the way," I said.

"Eh?" said the baron.

"There's a village at the bottom of the hill," I said. "You could ask a villager to take the invitation up to Sir Roland."

"That would certainly save time," smiled the baron. "But how do I know if some random villager will actually deliver the invitation?"

35

KNIGHTMARE

"Tell them Sir Roland will be angry if he doesn't get it," I said. "That should do the trick."

The baron nodded. "Good idea," he said. "Thank you, young Cedric. Oh, and talking of being angry, I forgot to tell Sir Percy that the king's favourite dish is peacock pie. His Majesty will be very cross if he doesn't get it. Farewell!"

Eek! I suddenly remembered I had a royal banquet to organize. I took the road back to Castle Bombast this time and collected Gristle on the way. As I strode along I wondered who would be angrier. The king if he didn't get his peacock pie? Or Sir Roland when he

KNIGHTMARE

opened a scroll from the king to find a two-for-one offer on Master Botolph's Bottom-Boil Balsam?

MASTER BOTOLPH'S
BOTTOM-BOIL BALSAM

Spots on the Bot?
Say Bye to the Lot
For a Penny a Pot!

SPECIAL OFFER:
Buy One Get One Free
While stocks last

Made from only the finest mashed slugs

Chapter Three

Peacock Pie
Palaver

"No!"

"Please?" I begged.

"No way."

"Pretty please?"

Margaret glared at me over the pot of
stoat and turnip stew she was stirring for
Sir Percy's supper. He still wasn't back from
the village.

KNIGHTMARE

"I said no," she barked, shaking her head so much that several drops of sweat flew off the end of her red nose and plopped into the stew. "I ain't cooking no fancy rubbish. Even if I wanted to, the master couldn't afford it. He ain't got a brass farthing left after paying for that bloomin' tapestry."

After returning from Sir Spencer's, I'd dashed to the kitchen to discuss the banquet menu with Mouldybun Margaret, Sir Percy's cook. Actually there wasn't much of a discussion. Margaret isn't exactly the top chef in the kingdom. Her idea of a banquet fit for Their Majesties looked like this:

Starter
Turnip Salad

Main Course
Crow and Cabbage Stew

Choice of Puddings
Cabbage and Turnip Turnover

– or –

Porridge

Yum!

"Sir Percy can't be *that* skint," I said. "He's just bought an expensive new hunting cap."

"Well, I dunno how he paid for it," grumbled Margaret. "And I dunno how he's going to pay for this banquet, neither. Peacock pie indeed!"

"But it's the king's favourite dish!"

KNIGHTMARE

I pleaded. "If he doesn't get it he'll be really annoyed with Sir Percy!"

"Ced's right," said Patchcoat the jester, who was in the kitchen trying out a few new jokes on Margaret. "Didn't you hear about the time the king stayed with Sir Nigel de Ninkham-Poope?"

"No," I said. "What happened?"

"Sir Nigel's jester told me all about it," Patchcoat went on. "The cook dozed off and burned the king's peacock pie to a crisp. What a waste!"

"Gosh," I said. "So what did the king do to Sir Nigel?"

"Well, the king was all very nice about it," said Patchcoat. "Told Sir Nigel not to

41

worry, it was a mere trifle, that kind of thing."

"Trifle?" said Margaret. "I thought you said it were a peacock pie?"

"No, I mean – well, never mind," said Patchcoat. "But then, a week later, the king suddenly announced that he wanted a bear for the royal zoo. And guess who was given the honour of going into the depths of Grimwood to catch it? Sir Nigel."

"Yikes!" I said. "Did he come back alive?"

"Oh, Sir Nigel is alive all right," said Patchcoat. "He just sent his squire instead. He's buried not far from here. The bits they found, anyway. What's wrong, Ced? You look a bit pale."

KNIGHTMARE

I turned to Margaret.

"Are you *sure* you can't cook a peacock pie?" I said weakly.

"Sir Percy ain't even got any peacocks, and that's just for starters," grumbled Margaret.

KNIGHTMARE

"I thought it was for the main course?" quipped Patchcoat.

"Less o' your cheek, Master Patchcoat," she snapped. "We can't afford a peacock pie and that's that. Now, I'm busy, so you two can clear off out of my kitchen. Unless you fancy helpin' me polish up the master's best silver plates for the banquet?"

"No thanks," said Patchcoat. "I think I'll practise my jokes in the castle gardens. Coming, Ced?"

"Er – all right," I said, following him. "But I can't stay long. I've got tons to do before tomorrow. It's not just the food for the banquet. Sir Percy wants me to sort out all the entertainment as well."

KNIGHTMARE

"Eh?" said Patchcoat. "Why didn't you say so? If you need an evening of amusement I happen to know the very person."

"Really?" I said eagerly. "Who?"

"*Me*, of course!" said the jester. "I've always wanted to try out a few jokes on a royal audience."

"Er – don't you think the king and queen might want more than just a few jokes?" I said. "Even if they're brilliant ones like yours," I added quickly.

"Don't worry, Ced," grinned Patchcoat. "We'll give them a right royal feast of fun. But I might just do a few gags to warm them up."

"Thanks, Patchcoat," I said. "It would be great if you could help."

"That's settled then," said Patchcoat. "Leave it to me."

"Cedric!"

I turned to see Sir Percy coming up the garden path. He had the (now empty) leather sack over one shoulder and a big

46

grin on his face.

"He looks very pleased with himself," said Patchcoat. "Where's he been?"

"The village," I said. "Something to do with the banquet."

"Really? So what's with the empty sack?" said Patchcoat. "Doesn't look like he's done much shopping."

Sir Percy reached us before I could answer. "Ah, there you are," he said. "Now run along, Patchcoat. I need to talk to Cedric in private."

"Yes, Sir Percy," said Patchcoat. "See ya, Ced. And by the way, why is a measuring stick like a king?"

"I don't know," I said.

"They're both rulers!"

Patchcoat wandered off, tittering to himself.

Sir Percy looked around to make sure we were alone. "So, did you manage to take it?" he hissed. "The invitation?"

"Yes, Sir Percy."

"Excellent! Good work, Cedric," he said. "Now I can look forward to the banquet without worrying about Sir Roland showing up to spoil the fun. I can't wait!"

"Oh, that reminds me, Sir Percy," I said. "Sir Spencer told me what colours he's wearing tomorrow. Just so you won't clash."

"Good old Spence," said Sir Percy. "He really needn't worry, though, as I shall be wearing a tunic in the *very* latest fashion. Orange and green velvet."

"But that's what Sir Spencer's wearing!" I said.

Sir Percy stared at me in horror. "But – that's impossible!" he spluttered. "I mean, he can't… Oh, bother! Cedric, I've just realized something I – er – forgot to do in the village. Tell Margaret to keep my supper warm."

"Yes, Sir Percy," I said.

As he turned and hurried off, I had an idea. Today was market day. Why not nip into the village myself and see if I could *buy* a peacock pie?

Suddenly Margaret came hurtling

towards me in a panic. "Master Cedric!"
she shrieked. "Fetch Sir Percy! Quick!"

"I think he's just left for the village
again," I said. "Why, what's happened?"

"It's the silver plates!" she panted. "Half
of 'em's disappeared! There's a thief in
the castle!"

Chapter Four

Market Day
Mayhem

"Are you sure someone's stolen them?" I said.

"Course I am," Margaret snapped.
"Come and see for yerself."

I sighed and followed her into the Great
Hall, where Sir Percy's family silver was
kept in a chest for special occasions.

"See!" she said, pointing to the open
chest. "There was twenty plates yesterday.

But I came in to polish 'em just now and there's only fifteen."

"You mean ten," I said.

"Eh?" said Margaret. "You sayin' I can't count?"

"No, no," I said hastily. "You're brilliant at counting." *As long as it isn't over five,* I thought. "But there are definitely only ten plates. Look."

Margaret counted them out on her fingers. She gasped. "Aargh!" she said.

"That's another five gorn!"

Margaret insisted that five more plates had just been stolen, in broad daylight, in the last ten minutes.

I felt sure she was mistaken. But in any case there wasn't much we could do about it before Sir Percy came back. I might as well still go to the village and look for a peacock pie.

I left the hall and went to get Gristle — only to see Sir Percy coming out of the stables with Prancelot.

"Sir Percy!" I exclaimed. "It's a good job I saw you. I thought you'd already left!"

"Oh, ah, I – er – forgot something," he said. He swung himself up into the saddle. "Now I really must hurry. Urgent banquet business, you know. Toodle-pip!"

"But Sir Percy," I said. "Margaret says

there's been a robbery!"

"What?" said Sir Percy. "In the castle?
Good gracious! Not my new plumes, I hope?"

"It's the silver plates, Sir Percy," I said.
"We need them for the banquet, but half
of them have gone!"

Sir Percy was speechless. I wasn't
surprised. The plates were twice the size
of normal plates and extremely valuable.
They had been specially made for his
grandfather, Sir Peregrine the Portly, so
that he could have first and second helpings
at the same time.

"Er – the silver plates?" he said, squirming
in his saddle. "Really? Are you sure?"

"Yes, Sir Percy," I said. "Why don't you

come and—"

"Sorry, can't stop!" said Sir Percy. "You deal with it, Cedric. I'm – er – I'm sure there's a perfectly innocent explanation. Giddy up!"

Sir Percy dug in his heels and rode off, clutching his big leather sack. It clanked as Prancelot galloped towards the village.

I tied Gristle up at the Boar's Bottom inn and wandered towards the village square. On the way I passed a shop with a gleaming new sign that said "Master Silas Stitchett. Tailor to the Gentry".

I must remember to tell Sir Percy that there's a new tailor in the village, I thought.

KNIGHTMARE

The market was in full swing. There were stalls selling everything from cabbages and cakes to toad-eye tonic and earwax candles.

There were also several pongy pens where farmers were buying and selling sheep, goats and pigs. Not to mention cows – as I found out when I slipped on a freshly

KNIGHTMARE

plopped cow pat and nearly fell over.

"Tell yer fortune, sonny?" croaked an
old woman with no teeth, tugging at my
sleeve. "You will meet a tall dark stranger.
Or was it a stranger called Mark? No, hang
on, a small park ranger…"

"No thanks," I said. I shook her off and
pushed through the crowd.

KNIGHTMARE

"*Luvverly pies! Luvverly pies! Come over 'ere and feast yer eyes!*" bawled a stallholder, as I walked by. "Afternoon, young master!" he said. "Simon the Pieman at your service. Can I interest you in one of my piping-hot pies?"

I stared in wonder at Simon the Pieman's scrummy-looking pies and tarts and cakes and pastries. They looked and smelled delicious. And there, in the middle of the mouth-watering display, was a huge golden-crusted peacock pie.

KNIGHTMARE

Then I saw the price and my heart sank. I only had a few pennies in my money pouch.

"Sorry," I said sadly. "That peacock pie looks amazing. But there's no way I can afford it."

A voice called, "Hey, Ced!" and I looked up to see Patchcoat. "Fancy meeting you here," he said. "What are you up to, then?"

"Trying to buy food for the royal banquet," I said ruefully. "But it's a bit of a wasted trip. What about you?"

"Remember those travelling actors who called at the castle a few weeks back?" said Patchcoat. "Master Perkin's Players?"

"Oh, *them*," I said. Master Perkin had offered to perform a play about Sir Roland bashing Sir Percy. I'd sent them packing pretty sharpish.

"Well, I heard they were still staying in the village," said Patchcoat. "So I popped into the Boar's Bottom to say hello."

"But why did you want to see them?" I asked.

"The banquet, of course!" said Patchcoat. "A banquet isn't a banquet without a bit of theatre, Ced. I've booked them to do a little play for Their Majesties tomorrow night. What do you reckon?"

I frowned. "Sir Percy won't be pleased if it's about him being walloped by Sir Roland."

"Don't worry," chuckled Patchcoat. "After the tournament Perkin rewrote it, so now it's the other way round. It'll give everyone a good laugh. *Especially* Sir Percy!"

"Well, I suppose it might cheer the king up, too," I said. "He's going to be cross when he doesn't get his peacock pie."

"Yeah, I dunno what he'll say to Margaret's crow and cabbage stew. Anyway, I need to get a new set of juggling balls. I'll see you at the Boar's Bottom in a bit. You can give me lift home on Gristle."

On the way to the inn to wait for Patchcoat, I noticed a stall standing a bit apart from the others. A cluster of curious peasants crowded around it.

"'Oo's this then?" said one. "Oi ain't seen 'im afore."

"Dunno," said another. "'E's noo."

"Looks a bit foreign, if you ask me," said a third.

"What's 'e sellin', anyhow?"

"No idea," said the first, picking a bit of dried cow dung off his chin. "Oi don't like the smell of it, that's for certain."

I edged to the front of the crowd. The stall was covered with an array of shiny brass bowls filled with exotic-smelling seeds and brightly coloured powders. The stallholder wore a long purple tunic fringed with gold and a bright red turban.

"Good afternoon, my friends," he began. "My name is Ali. Please examine my wares. I bring you the finest spices from the East."

KNIGHTMARE

"East of what?" said a peasant.

"Just the East, my friend," said Ali. "You know, as in the Indies."

"Undies?" croaked an old man, cupping his hand to one hairy ear. "'E says this stuff is from his undies!"

A rumble of disapproval went through the crowd.

"Ugh!" cried a man. "Oi ain't touching nuffin' what comes out of a foreigner's undies!"

"Nor me, neither," declared his wife, wiping her nose on her sleeve. "That's disgustin'!"

Muttering and grumbling, the peasants all drifted away.

"Hello, young man," sighed Ali. "I don't suppose you want any paprika to pep up your pig's liver pie? Or some cinnamon to spice up your suet pudding?"

Now there's an idea, I thought. *If I can't afford a peacock pie, maybe I could just get Mouldybun Margaret's food to taste a bit nicer?*

"Do you have anything to make cabbage or turnip more interesting?" I asked.

KNIGHTMARE

Ali beamed and pointed to a small sack of yellowish-brown powder. "I have the very thing," he said. "It's called curry powder. A little bit of this will add crackle to the clammiest cabbage and terrificness to the most tasteless turnip!"

"Sounds ideal," I said. "But how much is it? I haven't got a lot of money."

"It's my newest spice," said Ali. "But it's not very popular. I'll give you the whole sack for one penny."

"Brilliant!" I said. I handed over a penny before he could change his mind.

"Remember, don't use very much," he smiled, tying up the sack of powder. "It's very hot!"

"Thanks," I said, taking the sack. It didn't feel hot at all. To be honest it wasn't even warm.

I was almost at the Boar's Bottom when a sinister figure in a long, black hooded cloak crossed in front of me. He looked about, as if to make sure no one was following him, then dived into a nearby alley. I watched, intrigued, as he hunkered down in the shadows. I couldn't see clearly because the alley was dark and his cloak was in the way, but he appeared to be counting the contents of some sort of bag. Then his cloak briefly flapped open in the breeze.

KNIGHTMARE

He was counting big
silver plates. And not just
any big silver plates. I
could just see that they
were engraved with a
peacock – the badge of
Sir Percy's family. It was
the stolen silver!

The cloaked robber stood up and slipped
out of the alley.

"Stop, thief!" I cried, and ran after him.

He gave a start of alarm and then he was
running, too, pushing aside peasants and
weaving in and out of market stalls. Luckily,
I was much smaller and quicker than the
thief and soon I was right behind him.

KNIGHTMARE

I reached out to grab his cloak – but then a large grunting pig suddenly came charging out of the crowd, followed by its large grunting owner.

"Come back 'ere, you stoopid sow!" puffed the pig farmer.

I was right by Simon the Pieman's stall – and the escaped pig was hurtling straight for me!

KNIGHTMARE

"My luvverly pies! They'll be wrecked!" cried Simon.

"Shoo!" I yelled, desperately waving my sack of curry powder. "Go away! Nice piggy! Shoo! Shoo!"

The pig hurtled closer and closer – and then at the very last second it veered nimbly away with a loud "OINK!".

"Phew!" I said. "That was close – OOF!"

The pig might have been nimble, but his owner certainly wasn't. He ran right into me and sent me flying into a big tub of herrings at the fish stall next door.

"Sorry 'bout that!" grunted the farmer, running off after his pig.

"Oi, out of my tub!" barked the

69

fishmonger. "You'll spoil all my fish. They was fresh caught only last week!"

Simon the Pieman helped me out of the slimy, slippery mess. "Thanks, young master," he beamed. "You saved my stall! I think you deserve—"

"The thief!" I suddenly remembered. "Sorry, Mister Pieman! I have to go!"

I sped off towards where I'd last seen the robber. I was sure he'd been heading for the back lane out of the village. But when I got there I could see no sign of him. Where could he have gone? I stood by the new tailor's shop and looked up and down the lane. But it was no good. The cloaked thief had vanished into thin air.

Chapter Five

A Thief
in the Night

Patchcoat was waiting for me at the Boar's Bottom.

"What happened to you, Ced?"

He pulled a herring out of my hood.

"Something *fishy* by the look o f it. Not to mention the *smell*. Pooh!"

As we rode home on Gristle I explained what had happened.

KNIGHTMARE

"I just don't understand how the robber got into the castle," I said.

"Do you reckon it's an inside job?" said Patchcoat.

"What, someone in the castle itself?" I said, shocked. "But they'd be stealing from their own master! Besides it's obviously not you, me or Margaret. The thief was at least as tall as Sir Percy."

As soon as we arrived back, I nipped into the kitchen and hid the curry powder behind a pile of logs while Margaret's back was turned. Then I went straight to Sir Percy's chamber. He was standing in front of his looking glass in a dressing gown, trying on his collection of plumed hats.

KNIGHTMARE

"Ah, Cedric, there you are," he said, as I entered. "Where have you been? I need you to help me choose a hat for the banquet."

I told him about my trip to the village – and how I'd chased the robber through the market.

"Really? The – er – market, you say?" he said, putting on a hat with a bright green plume. "Good for you, Cedric. Didn't catch him though, did you, eh?"

"No, I didn't," I said, surprised. "How do you know?"

"Ah – oh – I just – er – *assumed*," he said airily. "You'd have told me straight away if you *had*, wouldn't you?"

"Yes, I suppose so," I said. "But shouldn't you try and catch him *now*? Organize a search party or something?"

"No time, dear boy, no time!" said Sir Percy, trying the hat at various jaunty angles. "I have far too much to do before the king and queen arrive. Perhaps after Their Majesties have left."

"But what if the thief tries to break into the castle again?" I pleaded. "Won't you be upset to lose any more silver plates?

They're very valuable."

"Ah, yes, alas," said Sir Percy. "But after all, plates are only – er – *stuff*, dear boy. A noble knight such as myself has very little concern for such shallow worldly things." He swapped the hat with a bright green plume for another with a fluffy purple one. "Now, which of these goes better with my eyes?"

It was late by the time Sir Percy had decided which hat to wear. I helped him into his nightgown, and then fetched his warm milk and honey from the kitchen.

"Goodnight now, Cedric," he said. "You run along. I'll see myself to bed."

KNIGHTMARE

"Are you sure, Sir Percy?" I said. Normally he says he can't get to sleep unless someone (me) plumps up his pillows and tucks him up for the night.

"Quite sure," he said cheerily. "You need an early night, Cedric. Big day tomorrow, eh? Speaking of which, I need to make one more trip to the village before the king and queen arrive. Wake me early, will you?"

"Yes, Sir Percy," I said, stifling a yawn. "Goodnight, Sir Percy."

I went to my own little room and flopped on the bed, thinking about everything I had to do for the royal visit. I still had to prepare the best guest bedchamber for the king and queen.

KNIGHTMARE

And what about Mouldybun Margaret's
horrible banquet menu? With no peacock
pie my only hope was to add a bit of that
new spice I'd bought. And I'd have to do
that while Margaret wasn't looking...

My mind was buzzing so much I couldn't
sleep. So I decided to nip to the kitchen again
and make *myself* a warm milk and honey.

I left my room and slunk down the main
stairs towards the kitchen. The castle was
dark and silent.

Silent, except for – *what was that?*

The door to the Great Hall was slightly
ajar. I stopped and listened. There was
definitely a noise coming from inside. I peeped
through the door. *Probably just rats,* I thought.

KNIGHTMARE

But then I saw something move. A shadow, over by Sir Percy's chest of silver. It was the thief! I couldn't let him get away again.

I crept into the Great Hall and slipped as silently as I could past the long banqueting table towards the hunched figure.

Then I tripped on something. I managed to stop myself from crying out and bent down to see what it was. It was Sir Percy's big leather sack. Why had he left it there? And then I had an idea. A silly, crazy idea – but one that might just work.

Silently I picked up the sack and tiptoed towards the thief. When I was right behind him I held the sack open, raised my arms, and took a deep breath.

Here goes. Ready – NOW!

In one fast move I whisked the sack down over his head and arms.

"MMMPPPHHH!" The thief gave a muffled roar and dropped the silver plates he was holding. He struggled to his feet – and I promptly pulled the sack down to his knees.

KNIGHTMARE

"Got you!" I yelled. But the thief shook me off and started running – straight into an old suit of armour.

"MMMOUCH!" he wailed, as the armour collapsed noisily on top of him.

I lunged for the robber, but slipped on the spinning breastplate. To stop myself falling, I reached for the corner of Sir Percy's new tapestry. It came away from the wall and collapsed on to me, knocking over several more suits of armour.

"Help!" I yelled, but I was drowned out by the deafening din of helmets, breastplates, greaves and gauntlets clattering to the stone floor.

KNIGHTMARE

I freed myself from the tapestry and saw the thief blindly bumbling his way through the door and disappearing.

"Stop! Thief!" I cried, but I knew it was no use. He had escaped again!

Then I heard a loud CLONK! and I was surprised to see the thief staggering *back* into the hall. He stopped, groaned, swayed for a moment – and toppled on to the crumpled tapestry.

I gasped in astonishment as Mouldybun Margaret marched into the Great Hall in her nightdress. She was holding a large iron frying pan. It was still ringing.

"Gottim!" she said, as Patchcoat appeared behind her.

"We heard the commotion and came as quickly as we could," he said. "Blimey, Margaret, that was a fair old wallop. He's not *dead*, is he?"

As if in answer, a long muffled moan came from the leather sack.

"No," said Margaret, "but he'll wish he was when Sir Percy gets hold of him."

"Shall I fetch Sir Percy now?" I said.

"Nah, wait till the morning," said Margaret, tying the drawstring of the sack tight round the thief's knees. "This scoundrel ain't going nowhere. But we can't leave him here. You two grab a leg each and I'll take the other end."

"Where are we taking him?" I asked.

"Best place for him," said Margaret.
"You'll see. It ain't far."

Between the three of us we lifted the
robber. We lugged him out of the hall and
across the landing, to a flight of stairs I'd
never used before.

"Down here," she said. "I'll go in front."

It was tough work manhandling a
grown man down a narrow spiral staircase.
The walls and steps were slippery and we
were soon in total darkness.

"Nearly there," said Margaret.

"Good," I panted. The place gave me
the creeps. It was chilly and dank, and

83

dripping noises and strange scuttlings echoed in the darkness.

"*Eek!*" I yelped, as something squeaked and ran across my foot. I put out a hand to steady myself, but it just slid down the slimy wall. I fell forwards – and the next thing I knew we were all tumbling head over heels in the dark.

KNIGHTMARE

We came to rest in a big tangled heap.

"Everyone all right?" said Patchcoat.

"I-I think so," I said. I freed a hand and felt under me. "I seem to have landed on a couple of big cushions."

"Oi! Those ain't cushions!" bellowed Margaret right in my ear. "Gerroff me, will yer?"

Eeeewww.

Margaret gave me a hefty shove on to the damp stone floor. I looked around. A barred window let in a tiny patch of moonlight. In the dim light I began to make out strange shapes hanging from the wall.

"So, what is this place?" I said. "Is it one of the storerooms?"

"You could say that," said Patchcoat. "Except it's for storing *people*, not things. Welcome to the castle dungeon!"

I peered again at the shapes on the walls and realized they were rusty old chains and manacles. In one corner I could make out a huge scary axe with a curved blade. Even under all the cobwebs it still looked pretty sharp.

"Yikes," I shivered. "I didn't even know Castle Bombast *had* a dungeon."

The thief groaned again.

"Come on," said Margaret. "Let's get this villain locked up before he comes to."

At one end of the dungeon was an ancient door with heavy iron bolts. With a screech of rusty hinges, Margaret hauled it open.

"Sling him in 'ere," she said.

The cell was narrow, dank and pitch-black. We dragged the thief inside and dumped him on what smelled like a pile of mouldy, stinking straw. He moaned groggily as Margaret whipped off the leather sack, shut the door and slammed the bolts into place.

"Right," she said, wiping her hands on her nightdress. "The master can deal with him in the morning. I'm off back to bed. I've got a bloomin' royal banquet to cook tomorrow!"

Chapter Six

Curry Carry-On

I hauled the thief before the king. I had single-handedly captured the most notorious robber in the kingdom. As the master-thief was led away in chains, the king drew his jewelled sword. He ordered me to kneel before him. Then he touched the blade on each of my shoulders and declared: "Arise, Sir Cedric!" *Arise… Arise… Arise…*

KNIGHTMARE

Arise? I opened an eye. What time was it? The sun was pouring through my window. Yikes! After all the shenanigans of the night I'd overslept badly – it was late morning and I'd promised to wake Sir Percy early!

I leaped out of bed, pulled on my clothes and dashed to Sir Percy's door. I knocked but there was no answer.

I knocked again. "Sir Percy?"

Again no answer. I opened the door and went in, ready to say sorry for not waking him sooner. Once I'd told him about the thief, I was sure he'd understand. I only hoped he hadn't missed an important appointment in the village.

KNIGHTMARE

To my surprise, Sir Percy wasn't there. Not only that, he'd even made his own bed, which is normally my job. And his nightgown was on the bed, so he'd even got himself dressed. I usually helped him with that, too.

Sir Percy wasn't in the Great Hall, either. (All I found there was the mess from the night before, so that was another chore to add to my list.) He must have left for the village. His appointment was obviously pretty important if he'd got himself ready without any help from me!

I went to the kitchen to see how the food for the banquet was coming along. I arrived just in time to see Margaret scraping a pile of plucked crows (*eeww!*) and a mountain of cabbage (*yuck!*) into a large cauldron of water. Patchcoat was telling a joke to two large cabbages wearing crowns made from old parchment.

"Ced!" he grinned. "Say hello to Their Majesties. I'm just practising some warm-up gags for tonight."

"Just as long as you don't call them a pair of vegetables," I laughed.

KNIGHTMARE

"'Ere, you seen Sir Percy, Master Cedric?" said Margaret, chopping a turnip in half with a single blow of her knife. "Where's he been? It's nearly lunchtime. His porridge is all cold and lumpy."

"Even colder and lumpier than normal, you mean," quipped Patchcoat. He ducked to avoid a large slice of turnip that Margaret hurled at him.

"Oi! Less o' your cheek," she snapped.

"I think he went out early," I said. "He had something to do in the village."

"Went out?" said Margaret, offended. "Without a bowl of my delicious porridge? That's impossible!"

Patchcoat winked at me. Anyone who'd

92

actually tasted Margaret's porridge knew that it was *totally* possible.

"Oh, well, I may as well tidy the Great Hall while I'm waiting for him to come back," I said.

"I'll come with you," said Patchcoat. "I need to work out where old Perkin can do his play."

In the hall I pieced all the suits of armour together and hung *The Triumph of Sir Percy* back on the wall. Meanwhile, Patchcoat cleared a space at one end of the hall for the players. It was well past lunchtime by the time we'd finished, but Sir Percy still hadn't returned.

After a late lunch of bread (stale) and

cheese (mouldy) in the kitchen, I returned to the Great Hall to prepare the banqueting table for the evening. First I put out Sir Percy's five remaining silver plates – one for each of our royal guests, one for Sir Percy, one for Sir Spencer and one for the Baron. Anyone else would have to make do with our usual plain old pewter.

Then I went back to the kitchen to get the cutlery, including some newfangled eating tools called "forks" that Sir Percy bought a couple of months back. (Waste of money if you ask me. Why bother with forks when you can spear your food on the end of your knife? They'll never catch on.)

The kitchen was starting to fill up with

KNIGHTMARE

steam and the stink of boiling crow and cabbage. *Pooh!* Then I had an idea. All this steam provided the perfect chance to pep up Margaret's foul-smelling stew...

While she wasn't looking, I grabbed my sack of curry powder from behind the logpile. I quickly untied the sack and tiptoed up to the fireplace. Then, under the cover of the steam, I shook a bit of powder into the bubbling cauldron.

"Oi! Fingers out of my stew!" said Margaret. I was so startled that I jumped – promptly tipping most of the powder into the pot. Yikes! Oh well, it would *definitely* be tastier now. I hastily stuffed the almost-empty sack up my jerkin before turning round.

"Sorry, Margaret," I said. "I couldn't resist tasting it. It looks so delicious!"

Margaret smiled, then her face fell.

"Hold on," she said suspiciously. "You've got something up your jerkin. You been nicking my turnips?"

ROOT-I-TOOT-I-TOOT!

Before I could reply, the sound of a trumpet drifted through the window.

"Whassat?" said Margaret.

There was another *ROOT-I-TOOT*, closer this time and accompanied by the pounding of hooves.

KNIGHTMARE

Margaret and I ran to the window to look. Riding into the castle courtyard was Baron Fitztightly, plus two junior heralds blowing trumpets.

"I'd better go and greet them," I said. "I expect they've come to tell us when the king and queen are arriving." It was only teatime and the royal couple weren't due for another two hours.

I ran outside and bowed to the baron.

"Good day, Master Cedric!" said Baron Fitztightly. "Kindly fetch your master."

"Er – well, I *would*, your lordship," I said. "But I'm afraid he's – um – not here."

"Not here?" said the baron. "I'm afraid Their Majesties get very upset if their host

97

KNIGHTMARE

isn't present to greet them."

"Their Majesties, your lordship?" I said.
"You mean to say—"

"Yes," said the baron. "They're early."

I gulped as, over the baron's shoulder,
I saw a whole procession come clattering
across the drawbridge. In front rode eight
palace guards, while two trumpet-tooting
heralds brought up the rear. But it wasn't

the soldiers and heralds that made me gasp. In the centre of the procession was a splendid gold coach drawn by four magnificent white horses. It stopped right in front of me and one of the coachmen hopped down to open the door. As he did so the heralds blasted out a fanfare and the baron bellowed, "Pray welcome to Their Majesties the king and queen!"

KNIGHTMARE

I watched in awe as the king stepped down from the coach. He turned to help the queen, but she brushed away his hand.

"Out of my way, Fredbert!" she cried. Then she hitched up her skirts and leaped out of the coach.

"Better now, Malicia dear?" said the king.

"*Much* better," she said. "I needed a jolly good jump after so long in this rotten coach. My bones have been rattled to bits!"

The king drew himself up to his full height. "Greetings, one and all!" he boomed. Then he saw that it was just me. "Oh. Where's that old rascal Sir Percy, boy?"

I bowed and said, "I-I'm not sure, Your Majesty."

"What, boy? Not here to welcome his sovereign?" said the queen.

"Quite so, Your Majesty," said the baron. "Disgraceful!"

"Steady on, you two!" said the king. "Don't terrify the poor lad. After all, it's not Sir Percy's fault we left our last host early. I'm sure he'll be along directly. Why don't you show us to our chambers, boy?"

"*Must* we stay here, Fredbert?" said the queen sniffily. "It's a frightfully small castle."

"Don't fret, my dear," said the king. "I'm sure Sir Percy has given us the very best rooms, eh, boy?"

"Y-yes, Your Majesty," I stammered. "Follow me, Your Majesties."

Yikes! In all the palaver I had forgotten to prepare the Royal Suite, which was right next to Sir Percy's chamber.

"Slow down, boy!" the queen called after me, as I hurried up the stairs. But I had to get to the room first.

I reached the Royal Suite and flung open the door. The last king to stay in it was King Ogbert the Odd back in Sir

KNIGHTMARE

Peregrine's day – and it looked like it
hadn't been cleaned since. No way could
I let the king
and queen
set foot inside
there.

   I swiftly
shut the door
and stood in
front of it as
the royal pair caught me up.

   "Well? Come along, boy," frowned the
queen. "First you hurry and now you keep
us waiting. Open the door!"

   I desperately played for time. "Er –
perhaps Your Majesties would like to see

Sir Percy's new tapestry first?" I said brightly. "It's in the Great Hall."

"Thundering thrones, boy!" said the king. "You mean you've made us dash up here and now you want us to go all the way back *down*?"

Eek! This wasn't going well.

"Stuff and nonsense," snapped the queen. "If you won't open the door, boy, I will."

I thought she was going to push past me to open the door of Royal Suite. But instead she opened the door right next to it.

"Wait, Your Majesty!" I blurted, as she strode haughtily into Sir Percy's own chamber. "I wouldn't—"

"Wouldn't *what*, boy?" said the king.

"Er – that chamber, it's – it's—"

"Small and poky," said the queen. "Yes, boy, I can see that. The bed looks barely big enough for one. And someone's left a disgusting old rag on it."

"S-sorry, Your Majesty," I said, whipping Sir Percy's nightshirt off the bed.

"Now run along and fetch our trunks, boy," said the queen.

"Yes, Your Majesty," I said, bowing. With a sigh of relief I left the room and hurried to get their luggage from the carriage.

Then I went to help the royal coachmen with the coach and horses, and after that I ran around trying to find somewhere for the coachmen to sleep, as well as the soldiers

and heralds. When I'd got them all sorted
it was nearly seven o'clock. The time for the
banquet was approaching fast — and there
was still no sign of Sir Percy!

I went to the Great Hall to see how
Patchcoat was doing with his preparations
for the entertainment. On the landing
outside I heard a strange noise. It sounded
like somebody shouting. Patchcoat came
out of the hall. He'd heard the noise, too.

"The prisoner in the dungeon!" I gasped.
"I'd forgotten all about him!"

"He's woken up, by the sound of it," said
Patchcoat. "Come on, let's go and see who
it is."

I grabbed a torch off the wall and we

went down the steps to the dungeon.

"Let me out of here!" shouted the prisoner from his cell. "Who's there? Can anyone hear me? Let me out!"

Was there something familiar about that voice?

In the door of the cell there was a small iron grille. The prisoner was peering through the bars. He looked jolly cross. And no wonder. It was Sir Percy!

Chapter Seven

Royal Rumpus

Sir Percy was furious.

"Outrageous!" he spluttered. "A valiant knight, locked in his own dungeon! The humiliation!"

We were at the top of the steps to the dungeon, outside the Great Hall. Patchcoat had slunk off to continue his preparations.

"I'm *so* sorry, Sir Percy," I tried to

explain. "We thought you were the thief who's been taking the silver plates."

"What? Oh, well, if you must know I was merely, er, *checking* the silver," he said. "To – um – make sure the rest of it was still there."

I was just thinking that it was a bit odd to be checking the family silver at midnight – and why would he need his leather sack? – when Baron Fitztightly came striding down the stairs.

"There you are, Sir Percy," he said. "Where the blazes have you been? Why weren't you here to greet Their Majesties?"

"Greetings, baron," Sir Percy began, bowing. "I can assure Their Majesties that

I have an *excellent* explanation…"

"I'm sure you have, Sir Percy," sighed the baron. "And they'll be delighted to hear it later. They're dressing for the banquet right now. I trust everything is ready?"

"Of course, baron! Just as soon as I've changed out of these clothes," Sir Percy beamed. But then his face fell. "Oh! I've just remembered there's something I need to get from the village!"

"Don't be ridiculous!" said the baron. "There's no time. It's almost seven o'clock and Their Majesties are starving." With that he swung round and marched back upstairs.

"This is all your fault, Cedric," said Sir Percy. "Bashing me on the head and locking me up. Why, I've a good mind to—"

Sir Percy was interrupted by a knock at the castle door. I went to open it and in swaggered Sir Spencer. He was accompanied by his squire, who looked like a miniature version of himself – right down to the emerald-green riding cape and toothy grin.

"Hey, Percy!" he said. He swished off his cape and flung it to his squire. In one movement the boy caught it, swished off his own cape – and then threw both capes to me.

"Oof!" I gasped, only just catching them.

"Whoops-a-daisy!" drawled the squire. I glared at him.

Sir Percy looked enviously at Sir Spencer

and his squire. They were both wearing identical new tunics of green and orange velvet. Sir Spencer looked at Sir Percy.

"Wow, Perce!" he giggled. "Where've you been sleeping? A dungeon?"

"That's a good one, Sir Spencer!" said his squire, tittering behind his hand.

"Thank you, Algernon," smirked Sir Spencer.

KNIGHTMARE

Algernon!

"Hello, Spence," said Sir Percy with a rather fixed grin. "Delighted you could make it."

"Oh, I get it, Perce," Sir Spencer went on. "It's a fancy-dress banquet – and *you've* come as a scarecrow!"

Sir Spencer and his squire fell about laughing.

"Ah. Very amusing, Spence, very amusing," said Sir Percy through gritted teeth. "Now do make yourselves at home in the Great Hall. I need to – er – go and change."

"Really, Perce?" sniggered Sir Spencer. "I'd never have guessed!"

Spencer and Algernon headed for the hall, tears streaming down their faces.

Sir Percy made for the stairs. Before I could tell him that the king and queen were in his chamber, there was another knock at the door. I opened it and Perkin's Players bustled in with chests of props and costumes. I sent them to find Patchcoat in the Great Hall and dashed upstairs after Sir Percy. I caught him at the door of his chamber.

"Sir Percy, wait!" I called. "You can't go in there!"

"Don't be absurd, dear boy," he said. "A squire does not tell a knight that he can't enter his own room!"

"But Sir Percy—"

KNIGHTMARE

It was too late. Sir Percy opened the door and strode into his chamber. I tried to cover my eyes in time, but I wasn't quick enough. For one terrible moment I glimpsed Their Most Noble Majesties, King Fredbert and Queen Malicia, in their Royal Underwear.

There was an ear-splitting screech and then the king roared, "Great suffering sceptres! Sir Percy, what is the meaning of this?"

"S-so sorry, Y-your Majesties," Sir Percy spluttered. "I didn't know—"

"GET OUT!" shrieked the queen.

"Y-yes, Your Majesty," burbled Sir Percy, bowing so low that his nose almost touched his knees.

"NOW!"

"At *once*, Your Majest-OUCH!"

A jewel-encrusted hairbrush bounced off Sir Percy's head as the door was slammed firmly in his face.

"Sorry, Sir Percy," I said. "I tried to tell you. Their Majesties are using your room. You see, the Royal Suite wasn't ready, and..."

"Oh, don't worry, Cedric," winced Sir

Percy, as he rubbed the new bump on his head. "If Their Majesties wish to use my chamber, that's fine."

"Really, Sir Percy?"

"Yes. I shall simply sleep in *your* room, Cedric," he said. "But I shan't forget this. Because of you I can't even get into my chamber to have a shave, never mind change into something decent. Sir Spencer will never let me live this down. It's a dress *disaster*, Cedric. A fashion fiasco."

Sir Percy's door opened again. The king and queen stood before us in magnificent robes. I was so star-struck I only just remembered to bow.

"Still here, Sir Percy?" said the king.

"In that case you can escort us to the banquet."

"Personally I would prefer it if you *weren't* dressed like a haystack," said the queen. "But it seems we have no choice."

"Sir Percy, lead us to the Great Hall," the king demanded. "Let the banquet commence. And it had better be good!"

Chapter Eight

Banquet
Argy-Bargy

Sir Percy and I showed the king and queen to their seats in the Great Hall. They were obviously still grumpy with him and things didn't get any better when I served up Margaret's starter. She called it turnip "salad". A slightly more accurate name would be "peelings".

"Splendid weather we're having, isn't it,

KNIGHTMARE

Your Majesties?" said Sir Percy cheerfully.

"Hmph," snorted the queen. "Certainly better than the food."

Sir Percy gave a funny, high-pitched laugh. "Ha-ha-ha! Excellent joke, Your Majesty!"

The queen glared at him. "I *wasn't* joking."

There was a low rumble.

"Hear that?" said the king. "That

was my tummy. When's the main course coming, Sir Percy? I'm so hungry I could eat a horse."

"Probably be a lot tastier than this muck," said the queen.

"Ah. Er – have Your Majesties seen my new tapestry?" said Sir Percy, quickly changing the subject. "Rather splendid, don't you think?"

"It's all right, I suppose," said the queen. "What's it about?"

"Why, *me*, Your Majesty," said Sir Percy proudly. "It shows my defeat of Sir Roland in the tournament."

"Really?" said the king. "I'm not sure I *quite* remember Sir Roland falling off his horse."

Sir Spencer sniggered.

"Besides, the victorious knight in the tapestry looks like a smart and noble hero," said the queen. "Not a shabby, unshaven tramp. Now look at Sir Spencer. That's how a knight *should* dress."

Sir Spencer gave a gracious nod, somehow managing to flash his teeth, shake back his golden locks and show off his new tunic all at the same time.

At that moment, Margaret stepped into the hall and announced, "Main course comin' up, Yer Majesties!"

"At last!" declared the king.

I went to help her bring in the crow and cabbage stew.

"Smells slightly funny," whispered Margaret, as she handed me two steaming bowls. "I think I might've left a few feathers in by mistake."

"I'm sure it's fine," I said. *Maybe best not to mention the curry powder*, I thought.

The king and queen gasped as I placed their bowls before them.

123

"And *what*, pray, is *this*?" the queen said.

"Looks delicious, doesn't it, Your Majesty?" said Sir Percy. "There's nothing like a good wholesome stew!"

"I totally agree," hissed the queen. "And this is nothing like a good wholesome stew."

"Wholesome?" barked the king. "Well, it certainly looks like it's come out of some hole."

Sir Spencer guffawed loudly.

"Go on, Sir Spencer, try a bit," ordered the king. "Tell us if it's as delicious as Sir Percy says it is."

"Ah – of course, Your Majesty," said Spencer. He scooped up a spoonful, held his nose – and golloped it down in one gulp.

"Well?" said the king.

KNIGHTMARE

"Actually," said Sir Spencer, breathing again. "It's really not that b-AAARGH!" He suddenly clutched his throat and leaped to his feet. "AAARRGHHH!!!!"

"Good gracious, Sir Spencer," cried the king. "What on earth is it?"

Sir Spencer had gone bright red. His eyes were popping like a frog.

"AAARRRGHHHH!!!! AAAAARRRGHHH!!!!!!" he spluttered, hopping up and down and pointing frantically at his mouth. "F-F-F-IRE! MY M-M-MOUTH'S ON F-FIRE!"

"Don't just sit there, Sir Percy!" cried the baron. "Do something!"

"WATER!" wailed Sir Spencer.

"WATER!"

Sir Percy picked up a large jug of water – and hurled the whole lot in Sir Spencer's face.

SPLASH!

Sir Spencer stopped dancing about.

"Is that better, Spence?" asked Sir Percy innocently. "Do you need another jug?"

Sir Spencer shook his head. He flopped back into his chair and sat there groaning. His hair and his splendid clothes were drenched.

Sir Percy looked like he was trying not

to laugh. But then the king turned to him.

"Sir Percy, this is an outrage!" he thundered. "Are you trying to poison us? And where's my peacock pie?" He stood up. "Come on, Malicia dear. We're leaving."

"L-leaving, Sire?" stammered Sir Percy.

"Yes, leaving," said the king. "This is the most miserable banquet I have ever been to!"

"I entirely agree," snapped the queen. "Our room is terrible, the food's terrible, you haven't bothered to dress properly and one of the knights hasn't even bothered to turn up. What was his name? That great hairy one who looks like a bear."

"Ah, yes, Sir Roland," said the king. "Why isn't he here? I sent him a personal invitation."

Eek! Sir Percy glanced at me. "Oh – I – um – well, of course Sir Roland would have loved to come, Sire," he fibbed.

"Yeah, right," muttered Sir Spencer.

"But – he – er – um – he's got a tummy upset."

"Really?" said the baron sharply.

"A tummy upset? Is that all?" frowned the queen. "What a wimp."

"Indeed," said the king. "Seems a feeble excuse to me."

"Ah, well, it's a very bad case," said Sir Percy. "Nasty touch of the trots. How can

I put it? His rear is – er – exceedingly *dire*, Sire. Probably something he ate."

"What, like a *porky pie*?" said Sir Spencer.

"I've had quite enough of this," growled the king. He turned to me. "You, boy. Come up and fetch our trunks."

"Won't you stay for the play?" said Sir Percy. "I'm sure you'll enjoy it—"

"Silence!" said the king. "We're leaving and that's final."

"But Sire?" said Sir Percy. "Are you sure there's nothing I can do?"

The king thought for a few seconds. "Well, now," he said. "As a matter of fact there is something, Sir Percy. I've got just the job for you."

"Of course, Sire!" said Sir Percy.
"Anything you want, Sire."

"I'm adding a new lake to the royal zoo,"
the king went on. "I need someone to catch
me a couple of animals for it."

Sir Percy perked up. "Certainly, Sire,"
he said. "A pair of ducks, perhaps? Or
swans? Or maybe a couple of large
goldfish, or... or—"

"Crocodiles."

"C-crocodiles, Sire?"

Sir Percy went rather pale. And then
somebody knocked on the door of the hall.

"Excuse me," I said, bowing to the king
and queen, and hurrying to answer it.

KNIGHTMARE

To my surprise it was Simon the Pieman, smartly dressed in his best white apron.

"Oh, hello," I said. "Can I help you?"

"You already did," beamed Simon. "You saved my stall yesterday. I could have lost everything. We've come to thank you."

"Well, it was nothing really," I said. But I was pleased all the same. "How did you find me?"

"I heard you and that jester chappie talking," said Simon. "You said something about the castle and Sir Percy, and I just put two and two together. Me and the missus and the kids wanted to bring you a little – er – *reward*."

"A reward?" I said.

KNIGHTMARE

Simon called over his shoulder. "All right, folks," he said. "Bring 'em in!"

Simon heaved the doors wide open. Then everyone gasped as half a dozen sturdy boys and girls in gleaming aprons marched into the Great Hall. Each was carrying a large tray piled high with fabulous savoury pies, mouth-watering

KNIGHTMARE

cakes, tarts, puddings and pastries, and
several jugs of cream.

But that wasn't all. At the head of the
procession, Simon and his wife were carrying
a great platter. On it was the most splendid
thing of all.

A huge, steaming, golden-crusted
peacock pie.

Chapter Nine

An Unexpected Guest

"Great blithering battering-rams!" bellowed the king. "My pie! My peacock pie!"

He strode over to Sir Percy, ruffled his hair and clouted him on the back so hard Sir Percy almost fell over.

"Why, you scheming old devil!" he roared in delight. "What a fantastic surprise! So *that's* what you were up to when we arrived!"

"It was? I mean, yes, Sire, it was!" said Sir Percy brightly. "I had this – er – little surprise planned all along, didn't I, Cedric?"

"Er – yes, Sir Percy," I fibbed.

"And – and – of course! – that's why I had to pop to the village, right Cedric? To – er – make sure the peacock pie was going to be perfect for Your Majesty! Isn't that so, Cedric?"

I nodded, grinning so hard I thought my face would snap.

"Well, well!" guffawed the king. "He certainly had us fooled, didn't he, dear?"

"Oh yes!" the queen laughed. "For a moment there, Sir Percy, we really thought your terrible banquet was *genuine*!"

"Oh! Er – did you?" beamed Sir Percy.
"Good gracious! Ha ha ha! Perish the
thought!"

"Well, what are we waiting for?"
bellowed the king, rubbing his hands with
glee. "Let's tuck in!"

Simon and his family placed the trays
on the table, and the king and the queen
dived in.

"Ahem!" said a voice. Everyone turned
to see Patchcoat's head poking
through the stage curtain.

"Your Majesties," he
declared. "How about
a little entertainment?"

KNIGHTMARE

"Splendid idea!" said the king through a mouthful of peacock pie.

"Very well," said Patchcoat, stepping through the curtain. "Tonight, for your delight and delectation, we have a very special play. But to begin with, Your Majesties, where does a king get crowned? On the head!"

Patchcoat waited for the laugh. Silence.

"Here's another!" he said. "What's the first thing a king does when he comes to the throne? Sit down!"

The king raised an eyebrow. The queen sighed.

"Just one more!" Patchcoat tried again. "What has four ears, six legs and a crown?

A king on horseback!"

The queen yawned. The king took another bite of peacock pie.

"Thank you, Your Majesties! You've been a wonderful audience. There'll be more jokes later. Now, please welcome the admirable, the awesome, the astounding –"

"Get on with it, man," said the king.

"– the *amazing* – Perkin's Players!"

There was a round of applause as Master Perkin entered the Great Hall. He was dressed as a knight, with a wooden shield painted with a peacock.

"Psst! Cedric!" Sir Percy called me over, as Perkin stepped forward and bowed. "What's this play about?"

KNIGHTMARE

"It's all about you bashing up Sir Roland," I whispered.

"Excellent!" beamed Sir Percy. "Well, I don't know how you did it, Cedric, but – um – um –" he fumbled for the right words. "Um – well done. The evening has turned out splendidly!"

"Thanks, Sir Percy," I said.

"Your Majesties!" Perkin began. "I am proud to present the premiere of our brand-new production—"

He was interrupted by a thunderous knock on the door. I ran to answer it.

"Who is it now?" smiled the queen. "Another of your delightful surprises, eh, Sir Percy?"

KNIGHTMARE

I opened the door and nearly fainted. It
was a surprise all right. But not a delightful
one. Oh no. I stepped aside as into the hall
strode – Sir Roland the Rotten!

KNIGHTMARE

Everyone stared at Sir Roland. Sir
Roland glared at Sir Percy. Sir Percy
looked as if he'd been struck by lightning.
I gulped. How had my plan failed?

"You made it after all!" boomed the
king. "Good man!"

Sir Roland bowed.

"And how is your tummy?" said the queen.

"My *tummy*, Your Majesty?" Sir Roland
looked confused.

"Sir Percy said you weren't coming because
you had a tummy bug," said the king.

Sir Roland looked fiercely at Sir Percy.
"Oh, did he now?" he muttered. "Well, he'll
be delighted to know that I'm *perfectly* well,
thanks very much."

"Good!" said the king. "I'd hate to catch a dose of the trots. I spend enough time on the throne as it is! Get it? The throne? As in the loo? Anybody?"

Everyone laughed politely at the king's joke.

"Well, Sir Roland, now you're here, help yourself to Sir Percy's delicious banquet," said the king. "And you're just in time for a play!"

"Oh! Ah! Y-your Majesty," said Sir Percy hastily. "Perhaps we should have a few more – um – jokes first?"

"Later, Sir Percy," smiled the king. "I love a good play. Master Perkin, carry on!"

As Perkin returned to the front of the

stage, someone grabbed my arm and pulled me to one side. It was Walter Warthog, Sir Roland's sneaky squire.

"So, Fatbottom," he sneered. "Perhaps you'd like to explain *this*?"

He pulled a crumpled scroll of parchment out of his tunic. My heart sank. It was the leaflet for Botolph's Bottom-Boil Balsam.

"What is it?" I said, as innocently as I could.

"Don't try that with me, Fatbottom," said Walter. "Sir Roland was out boar hunting yesterday and who should come riding by but Baron Fitztightly?"

"Oh, really?" I said. "What a lucky coincidence."

"Yes," spat Walter. "*Very* lucky. The baron told us all about the banquet. He also told us he was going to ask a peasant to take this so-called *invitation* —" he held up the scroll — "to Sir Roland. Of course, if he'd done that, we'd have thought it was just some kind of silly joke. And we'd *never* have known about the banquet."

"No, I suppose not," I squirmed. "Good job you bumped into the baron, then."

KNIGHTMARE

"The thing is," said Walter. "*Someone* must have swapped Sir Roland's genuine invitation for this stupid leaflet. I wonder who that could have been, Fatbottom?"

"N-no idea," I said.

Walter pressed his greasy face right up to mine. "Well, whoever it was had better watch out," he hissed. "Because by the time Sir Roland has finished with him he'll have such a sore bottom he'll be needing a year's supply of this stuff!"

He crumpled up the scroll and stuffed it down my jerkin.

"Shh, you two!" said the king. "The play is about to start! Sir Percy, where are you going? Sit down, man."

KNIGHTMARE

"Er – nowhere, Sire," said Sir Percy, although it looked distinctly like he was trying to sneak out of the Great Hall. Given what was coming next, I wasn't surprised.

"Your Majesties, my noble knights and squires!" announced Perkin. "We proudly present – *The Ruin of Sir Roland!*"

Chapter Ten

Food Fight

"WHAT THE—" snarled Sir Roland.

"Shh!" hissed the queen, as Perkin began:

"My name is Sir Percy, a brave
gallant knight.
I've challenged Sir Roland to
have a big fight.
Here he comes now! I'm afraid
he'll soon see

KNIGHTMARE

> *That no one is tougher and*
> *braver than me!"*

The tubby actor playing Sir Roland lumbered on stage to a ripple of titters. He had a ridiculous false beard and several cushions stuffed up his costume to make him look even fatter. For the next half hour "Sir Roland" suffered a string of mishaps at the hands of the dashing "Sir Percy". Finally "Sir Percy" knocked "Sir Roland" off the stage on to a pile of brown gloop. With a great howl "Sir Roland" declared:

> *"Sir Percy is the best, it's true!*
> *Alas, I've landed in the poo!"*

KNIGHTMARE

There was a great burst of laughter.

"Brilliant! Bravo!" exclaimed the king, clapping loudly.

"Funniest thing I've seen in ages!" the queen squealed in delight.

KNIGHTMARE

Everyone except the real Sir Roland thought it was hilarious. With the king and queen there, all he could do was smile politely. But I noticed with alarm that he kept fiddling with the hilt of his sword, and turning a deeper and deeper shade of red.

"Hey, I guess that's why they call you *Roland*," said Sir Spencer. "Because you *rolled* in the poop!"

"Good one, Sir Spencer!" laughed the king. "Now, how about some pudding?"

"Of course, Sire," said Sir Percy. "But no cakes for Sir *Roland*, or his squire will have to *roll* him home!"

Sir Roland finally snapped. He seized

KNIGHTMARE

the nearest thing to hand
– a jam tart –
and hurled it at Sir Percy.
Unfortunately, it was at
the very moment that the
king was leaning forward to
take the jug of cream. With an
explosion of pastry and jam, the tart hit
the king on the side of the head.

Everyone gasped. There was a deathly
silence. Sir Roland stared in horror.

"So," said the king gravely, "you'd
assault your king, would you, Sir Roland?"

"Y-your Majesty – Sire – I-I…" Sir
Roland started to mutter an apology.

The king cut him short.

KNIGHTMARE

"There is only one penalty for throwing a jam tart at the king," he said in a dangerous voice. The tension was so thick you could cut the air with a knife. The king stood up. "Sir Roland, I hereby sentence you to – THIS!"

In one swift move, the king picked up a large custard pie and lobbed it across the table. It hit Sir Roland in the face with a loud SPLAT!

The king gave a great guffaw – and then everyone collapsed in fits of laughter.

"I say!" said Sir Percy between giggles. "Sir Roland's been remanded in custardy!"

KNIGHTMARE

"What a terrible joke!" laughed the king. "You're almost as bad as that jester of yours. Take that, Sir Percy!"

He hurled an apple pie at Sir Percy – who promptly ducked. The pie exploded all over the queen's crown.

"My crown!" she yelped. "I'll get you for that, Fredbert!"

She flicked a ladleful of cream across the table, but the king skilfully dodged behind Sir Spencer, who took half of it in the left ear. The other half splattered all over Algernon.

"My outfit!" they wailed together.

"Missed!" said the king. "Come on everyone. Feast fight!"

KNIGHTMARE

Within a few seconds there was utter
mayhem as pies, cakes, tarts and puddings
were flying all around the Great Hall. Soon
even Perkin's Players were hurling food, and
all the actors gave a huge cheer when the
baron tried to dodge Master Perkin's cream
puff and fell bottom-first into a giant trifle.

KNIGHTMARE

Amid all the chaos I spotted Sir Roland creeping up behind Sir Percy with a large blackberry tart in one hand and a wobbling pink blancmange in the other. I was about to call, "Look out, Sir Percy!" but had to swerve to avoid a large dollop of custard thrown (complete with bowl) by Walter.

KNIGHTMARE

"Percy!" roared Sir Roland. "This'll teach you not to insult me!"

Then, as Sir Roland ran past a suit of armour, a leg shot out and tripped him up. He gave a great "Whaaaaa!" and fell headlong, sending both his missiles high into the air. They landed one after another on Walter, who was aiming another bowl of custard at my head. Patchcoat slipped out from behind the armour and gave me a big thumbs up.

"What fun!" said the king, clapping Sir Percy on the back. "I've never enjoyed myself so much in my life."

"Nor me," said the queen. "This has been the best banquet ever. Thank you, Sir Percy!"

KNIGHTMARE

"Nothing but the best for Your Majesties!" said Sir Percy with a bow. "It's all down to my perfect party planning!"

It was well after midnight when we saw the guests to bed. Tired, happy and covered from head to toe in dessert, the king and queen went up to Sir Percy's chamber. Sir Roland had already ridden home, vowing revenge for the way Sir Percy had insulted him.

"Saddle the horses, Walter," he'd growled. "I don't care how far it is, we're going home."

"But it's dark, Sir Roland!" whined Walter.

"What? Are you saying I'm scared of the dark, Wimpface?" he roared. "The dark is scared of ME! I'm not staying another second under Percy's roof!"

Wimpface. Nice one, Sir Roland!

Sir Percy had my bedroom, but Patchcoat said I could sleep in his small room off the kitchen. The baron and Sir Spencer – despite much grumbling – had to share the dusty bed in the Royal Suite, while Perkin's Players made themselves as comfortable as they could in the Great Hall.

I went to help Sir Percy out of his sticky, splattered clothes.

"Just one more thing, Cedric," yawned Sir Percy, as I tucked him up in my bed. I thought he was going to say something like, *Thanks for all your help* and *If it hadn't*

KNIGHTMARE

been for you I'd be off catching crocodiles.
"Bring me some warm milk and honey,
would you? And don't forget to tidy up."

On the way down to the kitchen I looked
into the Great Hall. The tapestry had fallen
off the wall again during the food fight and
the players were using it like a big blanket.
Half of them were already snoring while
others cracked jokes and helped themselves
to all the leftovers.

KNIGHTMARE

The clearing up would have to wait till the morning. But I thought I'd better just gather up Sir Percy's silver plates – after all, that thief was still on the loose.

I was on my way back to the kitchen with the plates when there was a knock at the castle door.

Who can that be at this time of night? I thought wearily.

It was a small man with a beard and eye-glasses. He was carrying a large bundle under one arm.

KNIGHTMARE

"Yes?" I said.

"Evenin'," said the man. "My name is Master Silas Stitchett." I was sure I'd come across that name before. "Sir Percy's new tailor."

"I didn't even know Sir Percy *had* a new tailor," I said. Most of the local tailors refused to work for him because they never got paid.

"I haven't been in the village long," said Master Stitchett. He patted his bundle. "This is Sir Percy's new velvet evening outfit. He came an' ordered it yesterday and was supposed to collect it this morning. But he never showed up."

So that was Sir Percy's "important

business" in the village! He was making sure he had some posh new clothes – while I did all the hard work.

"What a palaver!" Master Stitchett went on. "I've worked me fingers to the bone. First he comes along yesterday morning and pays me to make him a green and orange tunic. Wants it by tonight, he says, for some posh do. Then he comes back at lunchtime and changes his mind. Can I make him a gold and purple tunic instead? I says to him, gold and purple's twice the price so you'll have to pay double. He gets a bit stroppy, but in the end he agrees to bring me the other half of the payment this morning. And does he? No! But if he wants

162

this here new tunic he'll have to cough up."

I suddenly remembered where I'd seen Master Stitchett's name. It was when I'd arrived at the market. And then later on, when I'd been chasing the thief. He'd disappeared into thin air close to Master Stitchett's shop…

Something went *ker-plunk* in my head. It was the sound of a penny dropping.

"Hold on," I said. "Exactly *how* has Sir Percy been paying you?"

"Silver plates," said Master Stitchett. "Just like them ones you're holding. How many you got there? Five? Why, that's exactly what he owes me! They'll do very nicely, thanks." He put the bundle at my feet and took the plates from me. I was too flabbergasted to say a word as he tucked them under his arm, nodded goodnight and set off in the moonlight back to the village.

Sir Percy, I thought, *you might not owe the tailor any more. But you owe me. Big time. Again.*

I went back to the kitchen to tell Patchcoat the whole story.

"Hear that, Margaret?" he laughed. "That so-called thief of yours was the master all along!"

"Easy mistake t'make, if you asks me," tutted Margaret. Despite the late hour she was still up, stirring a pot of something over the fire. "What with 'im sneakin'

about all suspiciously like. Fancy sellin' off
his own silver!"

"By the way," I said to Patchcoat.
"Thanks for helping with the entertainment."

"No probs, Ced," smiled Patchcoat.
"I reckon my jokes went down a treat with
Their Majesties, don't you? Now, anyone
fancy some leftovers?"

I suddenly realized that I'd been so busy
all night I'd had no time to eat anything.

"Yes please!" I said. "But I think Perkin's
Players have scoffed the lot."

"Leftovers?" said Margaret. "Who needs
leftovers when I've made a nice big pot of
special porridge?" She plonked two bowls
down in front of us.

"Er – thanks, Margaret," I said.

"So why is it special?" asked Patchcoat, eyeing the porridge warily.

"I made it with *sugar*," said Margaret. "Go on, taste it."

"Sugar's expensive," I said. "Did you get it from the market?" I had to admit that for once the porridge didn't *look* too bad. I hungrily swallowed a big mouthful.

"Oh no," grinned Margaret. "I found it. Over there, behind the logs. In a sack. Must've forgotten we had some!"

Uh-oh.

"Um, I don't think that was sugar, Margaret," I said. "I think it was cur— AAAARRGHH!!!!"

Take a peek at an extract from
Cedric's next adventure:

Damsel Disaster!

Toot! Toot-TOOT!

Toot! Toot-TOOOOT!

"Ah, there's the post!" said Sir Percy.

"Splendid! Run along and fetch it, Cedric."

"Yes, Sir Percy."

I quickly finished strapping the last bit
of armour to my master's leg and hurried
out of the stables to the castle gate.

"Mornin', Master Cedric," said the messenger, tucking his post horn back into his belt. "Fair bit of post for Sir Percy today."

He handed over a pile of parchment scrolls. A few looked suspiciously like fan mail from Sir Percy's female admirers. One was tied up with pink ribbons. Another had little red love hearts drawn all over it (bleurgh). But most of them were bills with things like PAY NOW! and FINAL DEMAND – THIS TIME I REALLY MEAN IT! on them in big red letters.

"Thanks," I said, turning to go.

"Wait, Master Cedric!" the messenger said. "There's this box an' all." He untied a long, polished wooden box from his saddle.

"What is it?" I asked.

"Search me," said the messenger. "Posh box, though, innit?"

I piled the scrolls on top of the box and staggered back to the stables, where my master and I had been preparing to ride off on a tour of the manor. Sir Percy said it was important for a knight to show his face to the locals every now and then. But I reckon he just wanted an excuse to show off his best armour. Especially after I'd spent most of the morning polishing it.

"Letters for you, Sir Percy!" I said. "Plus this box."

"Excellent!" said Sir Percy. He carefully picked out the fan mail and then brushed all the bills on to the ground with a majestic sweep of his arm. "I shall – er – *deal* with these later," he said airily.

I watched as Sir Percy eagerly undid the catch on the box. Was it a new sword? Unlikely. The last thing Sir Percy ever spent money on – when he had any – was weapons.

He opened the lid to reveal something long, white and fluffy.

"Look, Cedric!" beamed Sir Percy, taking it out. "It's my new plume! Magnificent, is it not?"

"A *plume*, Sir Percy?" I said. "You mean those are – *feathers*?"

"Indeed!" said Sir Percy. "They are from a giant bird called an *ostrich*. Terribly rare beast, you know. A sort of cross between a chicken and a giraffe."

While Sir Percy was admiring his plume I spotted a sheet of parchment in the bottom of the box. At the top of the sheet it said Pierre de Pompom's Prime Plumes. Underneath were the words FOR IMMEDIATE PAYMENT next to a *very* large number.

"How fortunate that this should arrive just before our little tour, eh, Cedric?" Sir Percy plucked the plume out of his helmet and fitted the new one. "There." He handed me the old plume. "Kindly return this to my collection."

"Yes, Sir Percy."

I returned the plume to Sir Percy's

special plume shelf in the Great Hall. As I headed back across the courtyard to the stables, I bumped into Patchcoat the jester.

"Morning, Ced!" he chirped. "Where's Sir Percy off to, then? And why is he wearing an extra-large feather duster on his head?"

I explained about the new plume.

"*Ostrich?*" said Patchcoat. "Blimey. I bet that cost a bit."

I told him the price on the bill.

Patchcoat whistled in amazement. "Phew!" he gasped. "For that price I reckon they should've chucked in the whole ostrich! Well, I dunno how Sir Percy's going to pay for it. Margaret's already moaning about how little he gives her for food."

Mouldybun Margaret is the castle cook. And possibly the worst cook in the kingdom, too, though no one would dare tell *her* that.

"Anyway," said Patchcoat. "I'd better be off. I'm going for a tinkle."

"Thanks for sharing," I said.

"Not *that* kind of tinkle," chuckled Patchcoat. "I've lost a bell from my cap. I'm nipping to the village for a new one. See ya later, Ced. Have a good tour!"

Coming Soon!

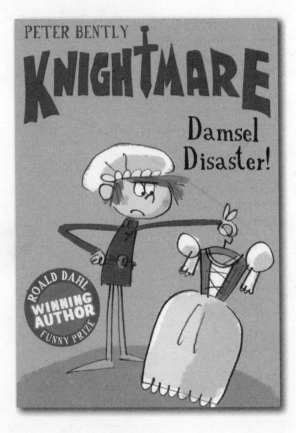